PUFFIN BOOKS

Warpath 3
Behind Enemy Lines

I turned to look at Billy. The excitement from having completed our mission successfully had left him. His face reflected the reality of our present predicament. Here we were, hundreds of miles from our own lines, with thick jungle in between. Our rations were low, so was our ammo. We were tired and weak. And on top of all this, 80,000 Japanese soldiers were looking for us, with express orders not to take prisoners but to kill on sight.

Read and collect the other books in the
Warpath *series*

WARPATH 3
Behind Enemy Lines

J. ELDRIDGE

A fictional story based
on real-life events

PUFFIN BOOKS

With thanks to
Wing Commander Ron Finch

PUFFIN BOOKS

Published by the Penguin Group
Penguin Books Ltd, 27 Wrights Lane, London W8 5TZ, England
Penguin Putnam Inc., 375 Hudson Street, New York, New York 10014, USA
Penguin Books Australia Ltd, Ringwood, Victoria, Australia
Penguin Books Canada Ltd, 10 Alcorn Avenue, Toronto, Ontario, Canada M4V 3B2
Penguin Books (NZ) Ltd, Private Bag 102902, NSMC, Auckland, New Zealand

Penguin Books Ltd, Registered Offices: Harmondsworth, Middlesex, England

First published 1999
5

Copyright © J. Eldridge, 1999
Photographs copyright © the Imperial War Museum
All rights reserved

The moral right of the author has been asserted

Set in Monotype Bookman Old Style
by Rowland Phototypesetting Ltd, Bury St Edmunds, Suffolk

Made and printed in England by Clays Ltd, St Ives plc

Except in the United States of America, this book is sold subject to the condition
that it shall not, by way of trade or otherwise, be lent, re-sold, hired out, or
otherwise circulated without the publisher's prior consent in any form of binding or
cover other than that in which it is published and without a similar condition
including this condition being imposed on the subsequent purchaser

British Library Cataloguing in Publication Data
A CIP catalogue record for this book is available from the British Library

ISBN 0-141-30239-9

Contents

The Fall of Burma

Burma was part of Britain's empire in south-east Asia. The British Military Command didn't believe that the Japanese would seriously consider invading it, so only a small force of a few British units with the locally recruited 1st Burma Division was allocated to defend the territory. Both were poorly equipped and inadequately trained.

In December 1941 Burma and Malaya (modern-day Malaysia) were invaded by the Japanese. They planned to cut the supply links between the British and their Chinese allies, as well as to secure a stronghold in south-east Asia from where they could control the Pacific. The success of the initial attack led the Japanese to increase the size of their invasion forces.

By mid-March 1942 the British in Burma were in full retreat, accompanied by thousands of refugees. The long journey back to India was one of the major Allied disasters of the Asian Front during the Second World War. At the end of May 1942 Burma was entirely in Japanese hands. The British had experienced a defeat which had cost over 13,500 lives and left Japan in firm control of its territory in south-east Asia. The Allied military commanders decided that Burma was lost and that the Japanese were almost invincible in the jungles of Asia.

One man was of a different view. Orde Wingate had successfully used guerrilla warfare tactics in North Africa in the early days of the war. He now proposed setting up Long Range Penetration (LRP) groups to go into Burma behind enemy lines. These groups would sabotage communications to cause major disruption to the Japanese. The way would then be prepared for an Allied invasion to recapture Burma.

Many of the military high command believed this proposal was doomed to failure. However, with the support of Prime

Minister Winston Churchill and the Commander-in-Chief in India and Asia, Sir Archibald Wavell, Wingate put together his LRP groups. In early 1943 he and 3,000 men (known as 'the Chindits') slipped into Burma against the 80,000 strong, so-far invincible Japanese army.

Our story begins with a young commando officer who quickly finds himself deep behind enemy lines.

Commando Supplies and Rations

At the start of the Chindits' campaign, each man of the 77th Indian Infantry Brigade carried a pack with enough rations for five days (consisting of twelve biscuits, 2 oz cheese, some nuts, raisins and dates, tea, sugar and milk) and one blanket. Instead of carrying tents, the Chindits built their own shelters on site from branches, grass and large leaves.

Each brigade had mules equipped with special double panniers made of thick solid leather, measuring 3 ft by 1 ft by 1 ft. These mules carried the vital signalling equipment. It took four mules to carry one set of wireless equipment, as follows:

Mule No. 1:

A radio set on one side, balanced with a spare set in the pannier on the other side.

Mule No. 2:

The battery-charging unit, balanced with two petrol cans in the pannier on the other side (when one of the two-gallon cans was empty, it was filled with water to balance the load).

Mule No. 3:

48 amp/hour battery on each side.

Mule No. 4:

Pannier on each side for other communications equipment (e.g., electrician's kit; oil for the charging unit; water and acid for the batteries; earphones; keys for transmitting; aerial, rope and spare copper wire; message pads; operating light for night work; groundsheet.).

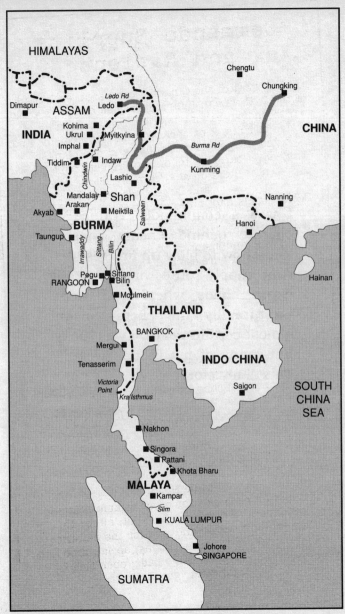

South-east Asia in 1942

I was a commando. Trained to operate behind enemy lines, I knew how to blow up bridges, disrupt supply routes and generally cause chaos wherever I went. Capture by the enemy meant almost certain death. I was lucky, but many of my friends weren't. This is my story.

John Smith
142 Commando

Chapter 1
Caught!

Night-time in the jungle. I lay hidden in the long grass. About fifty yards in front of me was a river, crossed by a rickety wooden bridge – a vital link in the Japanese supply line. My task was simple: to blow the bridge up. I was Lieutenant John Smith of 142 Commando. I was on my own because a large force would be spotted more easily than just one man. In the bag slung around my neck was my equipment: timer pencils, wire and plastic explosives, all wrapped in waterproof oilskin. I was light on weapons, carrying just my Colt automatic pistol and my trusty knife.

Ahead of me trees, bushes and long rushes lined the muddy riverbank.

I decided to attack the bridge from upriver. The current would take me downstream to the supports holding up the middle of the bridge.

Keeping flat, I edged forward, digging in my elbows and knees to zigzag like a snake slowly through the grass.

There were guards patrolling the bridge, the moonlight glinting on the barrels of their rifles. Ten yards to go before I made it to the cover of the riverside trees. Eight yards. Five. Four. Then I was among the trees. Crouching low, I moved towards the water.

Suddenly I glimpsed a movement out of the corner of my eye. Before I could turn and defend myself, a boot behind my knee knocked my legs from under me.

The next second I was sprawled face down on the ground, one arm pulled savagely and painfully up between my shoulder blades, the sharp blade of a knife pressed against my throat. A voice rattled out *'Sayonara!'* harshly before changing to a soft Scottish burr and muttering: 'That's Japanese for goodbye. You're dead, mate.'

Sergeant Ross stood up and let me clamber to my feet. He put his knife away and shook his head sorrowfully as he looked at me. 'Lieutenant Smith, ye may be a wizz at blowing up things, but ye still have a lot to learn about the jungle.'

After that first training session I walked back to my tent with my two pals, Cookie Watson and Billy McDermott. I felt humiliated and angry with myself for having been caught so easily – me, a trained commando. Billy sensed what I was feeling and grinned.

'Don't be so hard on yourself, John,' he said. 'It was your first day of jungle training.'

'It was your first day as well, but *you* didn't get caught,' I pointed out.

'That's because I started creeping through forests while still wearing nappies!'

Billy had been born in Kenya and spent much of his childhood hunting with his father in the African bush. As a result, he could sit for hours, hidden in a bush, barely moving, waiting for his prey to come along. Billy was small and wiry, his skin browned and leathery from years spent outside in the sun. His hair was black and thick, and with his pointed features he looked a bit like a jungle animal himself.

Cookie Watson, on the other hand, was tall and blond and burly, with a blunt snub nose, freckles and a perpetual cheery grin.

'So what if we can creep through the jungle better than you,' he added. 'You're the best at blowing things up.'

'It's important to me because I'm the lieutenant of this unit,' I retorted. 'I'm supposed to be in charge.'

'Who cares?' Cookie shrugged. 'Brigadier Wingate's in charge of the whole shooting match, but I bet he can't blow up a bridge as well as you can, or cook a hedgehog in mud as well as *I* can.'

Cookie had got his nickname because of his amazing ability to make a meal out of anything: hedgehog, lizard, even maggots. He could survive anywhere, he said, because the aborigines had taught him how. Cookie was from Australia. Like many others from countries of the British Empire, he and Billy had returned to

Britain at the start of the war to join up.

All three of us were the same age, nineteen years old, and had been together in the commandos. We'd trained in Scotland, where we developed the special bond that comes from working closely and depending on each other for your very survival. We trusted each other with our lives.

Reluctantly I agreed with Cookie: just because I was in charge it didn't mean I had to be the best at absolutely everything.

'Remember,' Billy pointed out, 'me and Cookie both come from tropical climes, but this is the first time you've been in the jungle.'

There was some truth in what Billy said. Most of the training missions I had been involved in had been sea-landings. This one was different. And we were also up against the Japanese.

'The way I see it,' said Cookie, 'the real problem with this operation is that we're going to be depending on so many other blokes who aren't like us. You know, who aren't trained commandos. Most of them aren't even volunteers: they're conscripts who had no choice about joining the army.'

'Not all of them,' I said. 'Anyway, the Gurkhas and the Burmese are all volunteers too.'

'Yeah, but they're not trained like we are,' continued Cookie.

'The Burmese don't need to be,' put in Billy. 'This is their home. They don't need training on how to survive in the jungle.'

'I do,' I said ruefully, still smarting over the way I'd let myself be caught by Sergeant Ross.

Cookie grinned. 'Don't worry, John,' he said, 'me and Billy will be with you. You just take care of blowing things up.'

I checked my watch as I slipped into my sleeping bag that night. Four hours to grab some sleep, then up at dawn for more training. As I drifted off to sleep, I could still feel the blade of Sergeant Ross's knife at my throat.

Chapter Two

Behind Enemy Lines

For the next few weeks we trained in jungle techniques at the Bush Warfare School in the Indian jungle. Along with learning how to live off the land for food, shelter and water, we continued to practise the skills we specialized in. In my case this was demolition. Blowing up bridges, buildings, trains, using the minimum amount of explosive to achieve the maximum effect. Anyone can blow something up using tons of explosives, but often they also destroy everything and everyone else in the area. If you're blowing up a bridge you have to know the bridge, be able to identify where the key supports are.

Everybody attached to our unit – the 77th Indian Infantry Brigade – was keen to knuckle down and learn, except Private Peter Parker. Private Parker was a conscript, and a moaner. He mumbled constantly to himself about how unfair this war was to him. Private Parker didn't want to be here in India, didn't want to be in the army. He wanted to be back home in Liverpool, painting roads and park fences and working for the city council. He wasn't happy out here. The reason I knew all about Private Parker's feelings was because he was attached to my unit.

77th Indian Infantry Brigade, also known as the Chindits, was made up of a regiment of British soldiers (the 13th Kings Liverpool Regiment); divisions of Gurkhas from the 3/2nd Gurkha Rifles; Burmese and Indian border men from the Karen, Kachin and Chin peoples, who made up the 2nd Burma Rifles; a section of mule handlers; and those of us from 142 Commando Company. In addition there were about a dozen pilots from the RAF who would be flying supplies in to us once we were behind enemy lines.

The brigade was split into seven columns, each one a mix of soldiers from all the different forces. Every column was divided into units. As well as Cookie, Billy and the miserable Private Parker, my unit had two Burmese soldiers, Ba Maung and Tig Kyan. They were both quiet men, fiercely keen to get back into Burma and rid their homeland of the Japanese. Especially Ba Maung, whose whole family had been wiped out by them when they had invaded Burma. All Private Parker wanted to do was go home.

After six weeks of solid training there was a new feeling of purpose at the training school. All of us, with the exception of Private Parker and his like-minded cronies, were fit, confident and straining at the leash to go into action. We didn't have to wait long. Late one afternoon towards the end of January, our whole brigade, all 3,000 men, was called to assemble in the grounds of the Warfare School for a briefing.

Most of us sat cross-legged on the ground, others found seats or positions on the low branches of trees. It was as if we were an audience preparing to watch an open-air show out here in a clearing in the jungle. The star of this particular show tonight strode into the clearing now, a bearded man, short and wiry. Brigadier Orde Wingate.

Wingate had a presence about him, there was no denying that. Everyone who ever came into contact with him remarked on it. The word was that most of the top brass, except for Wavell and Mountbatten, disliked Wingate. For one thing, he didn't dress up in a crisp, newly ironed uniform and parade around. Apparently one senior officer had been heard to remark that Wingate looked like he put his clothes on with a shovel. Nor did Wingate restrict himself to officer circles. He made sure he remained in contact with the ordinary squaddie. He was a man dedicated to soldiering, to fighting and winning battles.

Standing alongside maps hung from a frame erected between some trees, Wingate turned to face us.

'Well, men,' he said, 'I'm glad you're all fit and well and have had a good rest at this holiday camp!'

There was the usual laughter and groans that Wingate expected at this remark.

'I'm pleased to tell you that, after all the waiting we've all endured, we're finally about to go into action.'

He produced a stick and banged one of the maps.

'Burma!' he announced. 'Full of Japanese soldiers at the moment. Eighty thousand of them. We think we know where the big sections of them are, but it's difficult to tell with certainty from our reconnaissance because of the thick jungle. We're going to cross into Burma in columns, each column with a different objective. Our supplies will be carried either by mules or by ourselves. Contact between each column will be by wireless. We'll also use wireless to arrange for the RAF to drop supplies as needed, but you'd better make very sure of your position. We don't want the supplies being dropped into enemy hands.

'One of the primary aims of this operation will include cutting the main railway line between Mandalay and the Chindwin River.

'I have to tell you that there are no plans for getting us back safely. Once we have achieved our objectives it'll be up to every man to make his own way back to base here in India, or up towards the Chinese border. The Japanese will be hunting for us with everything they've got. But we can defeat them. And we can get away. Because we are the 77th Indian Infantry Brigade, the best damned force in the whole British Army!'

At this there rose a great roar of approval from the crowd, everyone waving their arms and cheering.

'We must all be as mad as he is!' grinned Cookie.

'Of course we are,' I said. 'Otherwise we wouldn't have volunteered to be here!'

A week later we were 130 miles away, at Imphal in Assam, north-east India, within 30 miles of the Burmese border. We had covered the distance in a series of night-time marches to avoid being spotted by Japanese reconnaissance planes.

At Imphal the brigade separated into its seven columns. Wingate had planned a multi-pronged attack, with each column heading into Burma from a different direction – some coming in from the north, some at different points from the west. The one thing every column had to do was to cross the Chindwin River which separated India from Japanese-held Burma. Our column headed due east into the jungle that bordered the Chindwin for many miles on the Indian side.

We spent the next two days travelling under dense cover. It was a tall order, trying to move four hundred men, mules and equipment through territory like this without being observed by possible Japanese spies in the area. All the time I had Private Parker just a few paces behind me, muttering under his breath about wishing he wasn't here. Billy suggested I transfer Parker to another unit and let them suffer his complaining, but I felt it would show failure on my part, admitting that I couldn't control the men under my command. At one point Cookie threatened to throw Parker into a swamp unless he stopped whining, so from then on Parker kept quiet and just kept a sour look on his face.

We came out of the jungle at a bend in

the river. It was about four hundred yards to the opposite bank. From our position we could see about three miles in either direction. That meant that if the enemy were hidden in the thick jungle opposite, they'd be able to see us cross. Once we were in the middle of the river in our small, unstable rubber boats, we'd be sitting targets. There was also the problem of climbing up the steep bank on the other side of the river.

'Ready, Lieutenant?' asked our company commander, Major Rawns, beside me.

'I was just wondering about the bank opposite, sir,' I commented. 'It looks pretty difficult.'

'Let's worry about that once we get there,' said Rawns. 'Send the men over.'

I got in the first boat with Cookie, Tig Kyan, Private Parker and coils of rope and equipment. A rope had been tied to the boat's stern so that it could be hauled back and used again.

Once we were away from the bank we had to paddle tremendously hard because a strong current dragged our tiny boat downstream. We were so busy fighting it that we almost forgot about the Japanese guns that might have been trained on us. Almost, but not completely.

Finally we made it across. Cookie leapt out and held the boat steady while Parker, Tig Kyan and I unloaded it. Then we tied another rope to the bow of the boat and signalled to our men. They began to pull the boat back with the stern rope. Three other rubber boats were making the crossing, their crews paddling at speed, confident that there were no Japanese lurking in the trees. Soon we had a make-shift ferry operating, using all four small rubber boats to bring a squad of sappers and their supplies across.

Now the work began in earnest. Getting a small group of sappers over was one thing, getting the rest of the men, the mules, and the heavy equipment was quite another. For that we had to bring thick cable ropes across. Meanwhile, the sappers were hard at work on both sides of the river, making rafts from any timber available.

Finally the thick ropes were stretched as taut as possible across the river, the rafts were ready, and the mass crossing began. Throughout the rest of the afternoon the rubber boats and rafts went backwards and forwards, the men using the ropes to pull them across. Those mules that were reluctant to swim were tied to the rafts and towed behind them.

While all this was going on, Tig Kyan and I were reconnoitring the steep and muddy riverbank, looking for the best route out. At last we found it: a small stream running off the Chindwin. It dried out after a few yards into an upward-sloping gulley.

'Here,' announced Tig confidently, pointing into the dense jungle above.

I hurried back and reported to Major Rawns. Then our column set off along the gulley in single file, every sense alert.

From this moment on we were in Japanese-held territory, behind enemy lines.

Chapter 3
The Deadly Jungle

At first light next morning our wireless operator made contact with Wingate's column, the brigade's mobile HQ. We learnt that four columns had made it safely across the river and, like us, they were now heading behind enemy lines. Two other columns, however, hadn't been so lucky. The one entering Burma from the north had been a sitting target for the Japanese as they'd tried to cross the river. Casualties had been catastrophic. About half the column had died while crossing. Those waiting their turn could only watch helplessly and fire at the enemy hidden in the jungle opposite, doing their best to try and avoid hitting their own men.

Another column, that had crossed the Chindwin about ten miles further north of us, had been ambushed five miles inside enemy territory. Fifteen men were dead. The rest of the column had been broken up into units. Most of them were now retreating back towards the river with the Japanese in close pursuit. The remainder were reported to be pressing on, hoping to join up with another column and complete the mission.

'Poor blokes,' commented Billy glumly when we heard this news.

'It's not all bad, though, is it?' put in Parker. 'I mean, for us it's a good thing. After all, while the Japs are chasing them they're not chasing us.'

An icy glare from me shut him up.

We broke camp, trying not to leave any traces of our presence, before setting off into the depths of the jungle.

Sunlight filtered down through the broad leaves of the huge teak trees as we marched. A light mist rose from the soft marshy ground. A peaceful scene if you ignored the fact that we were a fully armed column working its way across the jungle floor, alert for the presence of enemy troops.

As we marched the damp heat of the jungle clung to us, mixing with the sweat from our bodies. Our clothes stuck to us. All the time the flies and mosquitoes buzzed around us, crawling over our skin and biting. I did my best to swat them away, but after a while I realized there were just too many of them, so I let them get on with it.

It had been hot and humid in the Indian jungle. Here, in Burma, it was even worse. Without our acclimatization time in India, this jungle would have killed us with heat-stroke.

Keeping constantly on the alert, we marched through this tricky terrain at quite a fast pace. Now and then our column halted when the soldier on point thought he heard a noise ahead, or if there was a flurry of activity in the jungle to the side of us – usually only birds or animals we had disturbed. Our progress seemed almost too good to be true. It was. We hit our first major obstacle after three hours: a swamp of black mud that seemed to stretch for miles.

Taking the initiative, Johnson, one of

the sappers, edged carefully forward, making sure he trod where the rushes grew and the ground should have been fairly firm. He only managed three paces before he began to sink into the oozing black slime. Immediately the soldier behind him, Attridge, grabbed hold of Johnson and tried to pull him out. But he wasn't strong enough and Johnson sank deeper. Other soldiers grabbed hold of Attridge and a human chain was formed to haul both men backwards, slowly but surely. At last Johnson was pulled clear on to solid ground. His clothes were black right up to his armpits.

'Thanks, mate,' he muttered hoarsely to Attridge. 'I wouldn't have fancied ending my days in that lot.'

As the relieved Johnson recovered from his terrifying ordeal, Major Rawns assessed the situation.

'Right,' he announced. 'Two patrols. One to the east, one to the west. We've got to find a way round this swamp. Smith, take your unit to the east. Anderson, yours to the west.'

Steve Anderson and I nodded. Cookie,

Billy, Ba Maung, Tig Kyan, Parker and myself set off along the eastern edge of the swamp, constantly watching where we put our feet for fear of being sucked into it. After five miles we were still beside the swamp, so we returned to the column and made our report.

Anderson and his patrol joined us about an hour later with the same bad news: there was no way round the swamp to the west. We either had to go back and strike another route, or try to cross the swamp. Valuable time had been lost.

'How far do you think it is across this swamp, Captain Hayes?' asked Major Rawns.

Captain Hayes looked thoughtfully across at the jungle: 'Difficult to say, Major. A hundred yards across this first bit to those trees, at least. But who's to say what's beyond that?'

'Only one way to find out,' said the Major. 'One thing's for sure, we're not going back.' He turned to the rest of the column and called out: 'Right, men, we're going to make a causeway. Start cutting down some of the thinner trees!'

So we set to work, chopping them down and then hacking them into long logs. We spread these out on the surface of the swamp, criss-crossing them and filling in the holes between them with brushwood, branches and vegetation. Yard by yard we pushed out from solid ground, adding piece by piece of jungle timber and greenery to our causeway. It took us about two hours of back-breaking, wet and muddy work, but by the end of it we had a path of sorts across the treacherous slime. It took us another two hours to cross it, one soldier at a time so that the causeway wouldn't sink under too much weight. I was the third man to cross over. At every step the flimsy timber construction shifted in the mud and I thought it would give way. Understandably, the mules were reluctant to use it, put off by its unsteadiness. With some strong pulling and tough persuasion, though, the mule-handlers got them across eventually.

The heavier equipment was split between the four rubber boats. Then each one was hauled, slurping and slipping, across the swamp by a soldier moving as quickly as possible across the causeway.

At last, with every person and animal across, we set off through teak jungle once more. We had barely travelled half a mile when we hit another swamp. As before, there seemed no way round. Once again we set to work, chopping trees and gathering brushwood to make a causeway. Over the next four miles we did this six times. By the time dusk descended and we got ready to make camp for the night, we were bone-weary and covered in mud. The only lucky thing, to our thinking, was that no self-respecting Japanese would want to venture into this swamp-ridden part of the jungle.

Dawn the next day found our column already on the move. Each unit took turns on point. It was late morning when my unit moved to the head of the column. We edged forward cautiously through the jungle. Tig Kyan and I were at the front, Billy and Parker a few yards behind, and Cookie and Ba Maung bringing up the rear. Cookie, Billy and I were all armed with tommy-guns, the Thompson sub-machine gun, which had become standard issue for commandos. Parker, Ba Maung and Tig Kyan all carried Lee-Enfield rifles. I strained my ears, listening for sounds ahead which might give us warning of a Japanese patrol, but the thick jungle absorbed all noise. We'd travelled about two miles this way, moving slowly, guns cocked, prepared for an ambush. Then we heard a loud noise from straight ahead. It sounded like someone howling in agony. It was so painful, to listen to it made the hair on the back of my neck stand up. Aware that we might be walking into a trap, I gestured for Billy and I to go forward and for the others to remain at a safe distance behind us, but to keep us in sight.

Billy and I crept through the dense undergrowth until we saw a clearing up ahead. The howling was getting louder, more intense. We arrived at the clearing, but hid ourselves from view, our tommy-guns ready to fire at the first sign of trouble.

What we saw filled me with a cold anger. A Burmese woman was kneeling, sobbing over the bodies of two children. Behind her were the remains of a bamboo homestead, ruthlessly torn down. Scattered around the clearing were three dead Burmese adults. And tied to stakes in the middle were the bodies of four British soldiers.

Chapter 4

In the Drop Zone

The woman looked up and screamed as Billy and I stepped out of our cover. Then Tig Kyan appeared by our side and spoke in Burmese, which calmed the woman. Cookie, Ba Maung and Parker also arrived in the clearing and stood horrified at the sight which met their eyes. While Tig Kyan comforted the woman, I turned to Parker and Ba Maung.

'Report back to Major Rawns and the rest of the column,' I said. 'Tell them what's happened here and warn them that Japanese soldiers may still be patrolling in the area.'

Parker turned and hurried off into the jungle, the look on his face showing he was relieved to be leaving this scene. Ba

Maung followed, the fire in his eyes showing his anger and hatred at what the Japanese had done here.

Cookie, Billy and I surveyed the mess. It was pretty obvious that the four dead soldiers were from the column that had been ambushed ten miles north of us. They'd been trying to find us and come across this homestead. The family had given them shelter, only for the Japanese to track them down.

'But why kill the locals?' asked Cookie, bewildered. 'And why leave just her alive?'

We got the answer from Tig Kyan after he'd finished talking to the distraught woman.

'The woman's name is An Po,' he told us. 'What happened here is a message to all Burmese. The Japanese left her alive so that she could tell others what will happen to them if they help the British soldiers.'

Noises now came from the jungle behind us and we turned, guns at the ready, in case it was the Japanese. It was only the rest of our column reaching the clearing. The looks on their faces as they surveyed the scene showed the same revulsion that we felt.

I told Major Rawns what Tig Kyan had said, pointing to An Po, who was once again kneeling over the bodies of her dead children.

'The only survivor, sir,' I explained.

Rawns's face darkened with anger. He then composed himself and gave his orders.

'Deal with the bodies,' he said. 'Decent burial for our men. Find out from your Burmese what the proper rites are for their people and follow them accordingly. These people died for us, it's the least they deserve.'

'What about the woman, sir?' I asked.

'We'll take her with us until we come to a village where we can leave her,' said Rawns. Turning to Captain Hayes, he added, 'Captain, pass the following order along the lines. Whatever happens, in future our men are not to use local families for shelter. I won't give the Japanese the excuse to commit this kind of atrocity again.'

'Yes, sir,' said the Captain.

'We'll camp here tonight,' added Rawns.

34

'Send some of the men to check out the area for a good drop site. Then wireless HQ and tell them we'll take a supply drop at first light tomorrow. We'll give them the co-ordinates later after we've chosen the site.'

'Very good, sir,' said Hayes.

Ba Maung told us that the dead people had been Buddhists, so he and the other Burmese in our column held a brief but proper Buddhist funeral for their dead. We buried the bodies of the four British soldiers.

After the ceremonies I took Parker and Tig Kyan to find a good drop site.

Others set to work to make our camp. The unit split up to build temporary shelters from the surrounding trees and bushes. These shelters were usually situated about five hundred yards into the jungle, far enough from any path not to be spotted by passing patrols, but near enough to get into action fast.

Meanwhile the radio operator sent a message to Wingate's mobile HQ, giving a list of supplies we needed.

Dropping supplies by air was central to Wingate's Long Range Penetration strategy. He wanted his LRP columns to travel as light as possible, carrying enough food and ammunition only for four or five days. Supplies would be topped up with air drops. Accuracy on these supply drops was all-important. If our supplies fell into Japanese hands it could tell them many things about us: how big our strength was, our approximate position and what sort of weapons we were carrying. Losing our supply drop would also mean that we would be stranded in a hostile terrain, surrounded by the enemy, without food and ammunition. That was not a situation any of us wanted to be in.

At first light, exactly as ordered, two RAF planes came over and the parachutes with the crates beneath them floated down from the sky. We watched them from our guard positions around the drop site – a clearing, about five hundred yards wide, of firm soil, so that the supplies wouldn't sink into muddy ground. We were positioned around the perimeter of the drop site, guns pointing into the jungle, ready to protect our supplies should the Japanese launch an attack.

While the supplies were being unpacked and loaded on to the mules, Major Rawns called me into the clearing. He was studying a map of the area, with sections marked according to information gathered from local Burmese people as well as from those who'd fled at the time of the Japanese invasion.

'Right, Lieutenant,' said Rawns. 'This is where you and your boys come into your own.' He tapped a line marked on the map. 'This is our first objective, the railway line that connects Mandalay and Myitkyina.' He tapped another point, about fifteen miles north-west of the railway line. 'We are here. According to this map the terrain shouldn't be too difficult. We should be able to reach it by late afternoon. We'll make camp, and then tonight you'll take a unit and blow the line up. After what happened back there, let's do something spectacular. Show the Japs we mean business. Do you think you can do it?'

I studied the map, checking the route of the railway line. It was all on flat ground, which made it difficult. The best way to take out a railway line with any long-term effect is to destroy one of its bridges or tunnels. There seemed to be neither on this particular stretch, just a railway line cut through the jungle. However, I had one idea.

'I'd like to talk to the woman survivor, sir,' I said. 'If we can find out the troop movements along the railway line, we might be able to do some major damage involving more than just the track.'

'Find out and report back to me,' said Rawns.

I saluted and hurried over to where Ba Maung was talking to An Po. She still seemed to be in a state of shock, but Ba Maung had calmed her down, taking turns with Tig Kyan to keep watch over her during the night, such was her fear that the Japanese might return.

'Ba Maung,' I said, 'we're going to blow the railway line.'

'Kill Japanese?' he asked.

'That depends on what she can tell us,' I said. 'Ask her if she knows about the railway line. How often do trains pass along it? Once a day? Every two days? How big are the trains? Do they carry soldiers?'

Ba Maung saw what I was getting at and began to question An Po. When she realized that I intended to wreck the railway line, and possibly a trainload of Japanese soldiers with it, she was only too keen to co-operate.

Ba Maung discovered that a train came along the line every three days with supplies for the troops to the north. Usually there was one carriage filled with soldiers to guard the supplies, as well as other troops stationed at intervals along the length of the train. The next supply train was due the following morning.

I passed this information back to Major Rawns and filled him in on my proposal: not only to destroy the railway line but also to ambush the train.

'Pay them back for what they did to the Burmese family and our men,' mused Rawns. 'Very well, Lieutenant. But you'd better make damned sure you stop that train.'

Chapter 5
Ambush

We made good time through the jungle and by four o'clock that afternoon, according to the map, we were two miles west of the railway line.

Taking my bag of tricks with me, including my detonators, explosives and wire, I set off towards the line, accompanied by Captain Hayes and two hundred armed soldiers. I took Cookie and Billy as my back-up demolition unit, and three other commandos, Reg Johnson, Dinny Wetherall and Peter Simpson. Like me, Peter was a specialist in demolition.

My plan was to set two explosions a mile apart, wrecking the line. Peter would set one charge while Dinny and Reg gave him cover. I'd set my charges while Cookie and

Billy kept a watchful eye for me. Tig Kyan and six other Burmese were near by in case we ran into locals and needed a translator. The two hundred soldiers would stay fifty yards further back in the jungle, ready for action if needed.

As we crept towards the railway line I kept remembering Sergeant Ross's knife at my throat, and I wondered if I'd meet the same fate here. We crawled the last hundred yards on our hands and knees, making as little sound as possible. We were in luck: the Japanese obviously didn't think this piece of line was vulnerable to attack.

The stretch of track I had chosen was straight for about two miles. This meant that Peter and I could keep in sight and warn each other about any snags. The track also had a downhill gradient. I wanted this for two reasons. Firstly, guards were generally always more alert when a train was going slowly uphill, where an attack was more likely. Secondly, when the train came off the rails I wanted it to be going at speed so that the damage would be severe. I indicated to Peter where I wanted him to lay his charges and watched him set off with Reg and Dinny.

Billy and Cookie positioned themselves in the jungle on either side of the railway line, tommy-guns at the ready, watching out for any approaching enemy. Then I set to work.

I packed the explosive beneath both rails. While I was doing this, Tig Kyan came and scraped a shallow channel from the rails into the jungle. I unreeled the two lengths of detonator wire into this channel. Tig Kyan covered the wire and brushed the earth with some leaves so that it appeared untouched. I plugged the ends of the wires into the explosive and made sure they were hidden from view by taping them under the rails.

Back in the jungle I rigged up the detonator. It was quite simple: just the bare ends of two wires which, when touched together, completed an electrical circuit, triggering the explosives.

I looked along the line towards Peter. He raised his arm to let me know he had finished setting his charges. We were ready.

Soon it was pitch dark, so we settled down to wait till morning, and the arrival of the train.

When the sun came up at half past six we were all up and ready. I crouched beside my detonators. The two hundred soldiers were in the jungle either side of the track between me and Peter.

The minutes passed. Seven a.m. Then eight.

The time stretched into hours. Nine o'clock came and went. Then ten. Then eleven. I began to wonder whether An Po had been right about the train. Out here in the jungle, where time meant so very little, one day was much like another and it would be easy to get confused about timings. Maybe the train had passed here the previous morning and wouldn't be passing again for another two days. Maybe the Japanese had decided not to send the train at all. All these thoughts rushed through my mind as I waited there.

Noon arrived. The hot midday sun beat down on the railway tracks, making them shimmer in the heat haze. It was

43

sweltering. Sweat trickled down our faces and bodies and soaked our clothes.

Still there was no sign of the train.

One o'clock.

Two o'clock. No train.

Then, just as my watch was showing three o'clock, we heard the rails vibrating. A train was approaching. The news passed quickly along the two hidden lines of soldiers and immediately every man prepared for action.

The train was travelling at about thirty miles an hour. I could hear the engine hissing and steaming as it drew nearer and I could smell the smoke from its funnel. I wanted to take a look at it but dared not move in case I was spotted. I remained crouching on the edge of the jungle, hidden in long grass. The train came nearer and nearer. As I'd hoped, it began to pick up speed as it reached the downhill section. I could see the flatbed trucks with guns mounted on them and their crews standing beside them. Then came the supply wagons, followed by a carriage filled with armed Japanese soldiers and another supply wagon. All the time I was counting the seconds, working out the position of the engine. As another flatbed truck with heavy guns mounted on it passed, I touched the ends of the wires, triggering the detonator.

Chapter 6
Under Attack

My explosion was the signal for Peter to set off his. Both explosions were almost drowned by the screeching sound of metal on metal as the train began buckling, each carriage piling into the back of the one in front.

Our men were already coming out of the jungle, guns aimed and firing, but there was little need for a sustained attack: the explosives had done their work. The wreckage covered the twisted and buckled track. Two of the carriages had been hurled into the jungle. Dead Japanese soldiers lay everywhere, many of them trapped beneath upturned carriages, flatbed trucks and wagons.

It was all over in five minutes.

'Take the supplies from the wagons,' ordered Captain Hayes. 'Each man to carry what he can. Destroy the rest. Check our casualties.'

As our men disappeared back into the jungle, Peter, Cookie, Billy and I began rigging explosive charges to destroy the supplies that we couldn't carry. That done, we slipped back into the jungle and headed back to camp. We had struck our first major blow against the Japanese invaders of Burma.

Next day we put as much distance as we could between ourselves and the scene of the ambush. To gain greater mileage, Major Rawns decided that, for once, we would use the road that ran through the jungle. It was a risky decision and one that Private Parker complained about bitterly as we marched along at a fast pace.

'This is stupid,' he grumbled. 'Walking down a road. We could be walking right into a Jap camp. Or into a Jap convoy.'

'Not half as big a risk as if he let us go slowly through the jungle,' I responded. 'They'd come down this road and cut us off before you could blink an eye. Think about it.'

Parker thought about the consequences, and that silenced him.

There was no doubt that the major was right to take the risk. The Japanese would be searching for us with a vengeance, furious at the destruction of the railway line and the disruption of supplies to their front-line forces. Speed was of the essence if we were to get away. We could travel at a faster pace on the road than through the jungle. The other important factor about using this road was that we knew where we were on the map. Sometimes maps can be very misleading, especially when you're in the jungle. There are no particular markers and each swamp and each tree looks very much like every other swamp and tree.

We carried on marching right through the night, something else it's only possible to do on a road. Fortunately the moon was bright enough for us to see the way ahead.

I was worried that An Po wouldn't be able to keep up with us, but I had under-estimated her. Although she looked thin and underfed, she was fit and strong. I guessed it was the result of leading a hard life in the jungle. Ba Maung also stayed beside her during the whole march as her protector.

Soon after dawn a runner came back from the point patrol. He looked as if he was about to collapse. He'd obviously run the half mile from the front at a sprint, no mean task when fully laden with pack and rations.

'Jap convoy approaching!' he said. 'Point patrol's taken cover.'

'Right!' ordered Major Rawns. 'Everyone into the jungle. And no one shoots unless we're spotted. Let them pass. Understand? We'll make them think we haven't got this far yet.'

Immediately all the men took cover at least two hundred yards into the jungle.

We lay there, guns pointing towards the road, ready to be used if necessary. Ten minutes later the convoy appeared, heading, presumably, for the scene of the railway ambush.

Although we could have hit the convoy with ease, I felt Major Rawns showed great tactical skill in letting them pass unscathed. The Japs would think we were escaping through the jungle and would estimate our position to be further north. If they searched for us up there, then it would be easier for us to reach our next objective: the railway line to the south between Mandalay and Lashio. But to get there we had another major obstacle to face: the wide and fast-flowing Irrawaddy River.

For the next two days we continued south, keeping to the jungle. That fast march along the road had given us the time advantage we needed. Now there was the danger that the road would lead us directly into Japanese hands, so we returned to the shelter of the jungle, even though our progress was slower. We kept near the road in case we needed it.

On the second day one of the Burmese, Mek Ya, said that a village he knew was about four miles away. He felt that An Po would be safe there with his relatives. She was keen to get back to her own people, so Mek Ya and Ba Maung diverted with An Po to the village while we continued on our way.

When Ba Maung and Mek Ya rejoined us, Ba assured me that the villagers would take good care of An Po and that they would say nothing about our presence, because of their hatred of the Japanese and their fear of reprisals.

All the time we were receiving radio reports from Brigade HQ, updating us about the progress of the other columns. Apparently our attack on the railway line had had a major effect on enemy morale. Many Japanese soldiers were now afraid of the 'round-eyed barbarians' who might sneak out of the jungle and attack them. As a result the Japanese High Command had decided that we must be caught, to prove to their forces that we weren't some superhuman warriors, but just like them. The order had gone out that if we were caught we were to be interrogated and then killed. No one was to be kept prisoner.

'Death or glory, eh!' Cookie remarked when he heard this news.

'No glory for us ordinary blokes,'

commented Parker acidly. 'That's only for officers.'

After another day's march through the jungle we came to our biggest obstacle so far: the Irrawaddy River. It was much wider than the Chindwin and with a stronger current.

We crossed it in the same way as we had the Chindwin. My unit went over with the first rubber boats, our eyes and guns scanning the opposite bank the whole time. After landing, we sent the boats back for the sappers. Meanwhile men on both banks were cutting down trees to make rafts. Working in relays, about 150 men were soon with us on the southern bank of the river, including Captain Hayes. Major Rawns stayed on the northern bank, directing operations.

Suddenly the mules on the northern bank began to make a peculiar braying sound. I looked across and saw the muleteers trying to calm them down, but even from this distance I could see that the mules had their ears back, their eyes were wide, their nostrils flaring. The mules on the rafts were also twitchy They began to shift about, making the rafts difficult to control. The mules our side of the river caught the mood and began to bray and fidget unhappily.

'Something's going on!' whispered Cookie next to me. 'Always trust an animal's sense of danger.'

He slipped his gun off his shoulder and held it ready, aimed at the jungle ahead of us. His eyes scanned the dense trees for movement.

On the northern bank the mules had calmed down, but only because the muleteers were talking to them, reassuring them. A group of rafts were now halfway across the river.

Suddenly a hail of gunfire from further up the Irrawaddy hit them. The bullets shredded the ropes, cutting the rafts adrift. They began to rush downriver, bucking and tilting in the strong current, the bodies of the dead soldiers and mules tumbling off them.

The Japanese had found us.

The Chindits in Action

The following pages are actual photographs taken during the Chindit campaign.

Brigadier Orde-Wingate – Chindit founder

Chindit briefing at main base

Rations for ten days

Chindits cooking in the jungle

Chindits on the move

Mules take the strain

Supplies dropped in by air

Wireless operator

Preparing a bridge for demolition

Crossing the Irrawaddy

One of the last ever pictures to be taken of Wingate

Chapter 7
Deeper into Enemy Territory

Immediately those of us on the southern bank began shooting at the attackers upstream. They returned fire, bullets from their heavy guns smashing into the trees around us. Further along the northern bank, some Japanese units were closing in on Major Rawns and his men. We could only watch in horror as they were mown down. There was nothing we could do to help them. We couldn't fire at the enemy for fear of hitting our own men.

Rawns turned and shouted at us. Because of the noise of the gunfire we couldn't make out his words, but his gestures were clear. He was ordering Captain Hayes to get away as fast as possible.

I saw Hayes hesitate, loath to leave

Rawns and his men. Nevertheless, he realized, as surely as we all did, that there was nothing else to do. We heard the bitterness and reluctance in Hayes's voice as he gave the order to move off.

My last sight of Major Rawns and the men on the northern bank was of them firing into the jungle as they were cut down by heavy machine-gun fire. Major Rawns was among the last to fall. Then the jungle swallowed me up and I saw no more. But terrible images of the day's events stayed with me for long afterwards.

Under Captain Hayes's command we pushed on as fast as we could, barely even stopping to rest. Most of our mules had been lost in the attack at the Irrawaddy. Only six were left to carry the whole column's equipment. I requisitioned two of them to carry the explosives. The radio and its batteries were loaded on to the remainder.

Of the original 400 men in our column who had set out across the Chindwin, we were now down to 150. We were a sombre bunch as we moved through the jungle, aware that we were now deep inside enemy territory and that the Japanese were throwing everything at us.

We managed to radio Brigade HQ for supplies. Bang on schedule, they came the next day, parachuting down from the RAF transport plane. We didn't waste any time making camp once the drop had been carried out. We just gathered up the supplies, split them between the men, and then set off again. We didn't doubt that the Japanese would have spotted the parachutes descending and would be heading in our direction.

Over the next couple of days we received reports from villagers about the Japanese being in the vicinity, but we never bumped into them. It was a life-or-death, cat-and-mouse game played out in the thick jungle: large numbers of Japanese looking for us, and us keeping well hidden.

The Japanese were so determined to catch us that they even did a leaflet drop, thousands of leaflets cascading down from their planes as they flew over the jungle. We managed to pick up a few. The leaflets were printed in three languages:

English, Urdu (for the Indian men) and Burmese, and their message was loud and clear:

To the Pitiable Anglo-Indian Soldiery.

Your forces have been utterly destroyed in the battle of the 3rd March, and not a man has been able to recross the Chindwin. The powerful Imperial Army of Nippon is all around you and you cannot possibly escape. Do not again trust your brutal and selfish British officers, who will leave you to starve in the jungles as they did last year. Come to the nearest Nippon soldiers with this leaflet in your hand and we will treat you well.

I saw Private Parker reading one of the leaflets and gave him an icy stare. He screwed it up and threw it away, but there was no mistaking the thoughtful look on his face.

At our first chance to make a proper camp, I produced the map showing the Mandalay–Lashio railway line to the rest of my unit to discuss tactics. Private Parker made it clear that he wasn't keen on discussing any tactic except retreat.

'This is madness,' he grumbled. 'Over half of us dead, and it's just sheer luck that it wasn't all of us. We ought to head back.'

'Where to?' I snapped. 'Back into the hands of the Japanese?'

'They said in that leaflet we'd be treated well,' he insisted.

'Yeah?' said Cookie sarcastically. 'Like those four English soldiers we found in that wrecked village?'

Parker fell silent.

'Let's get this clear,' I added. 'We have a mission to accomplish. When that's done, or when we're given orders by Captain Hayes or Brigadier Wingate, then we head back. *Not* before.'

I then turned back to the map.

'Right,' I said. 'Let's work out the best place to blow this line.'

Cookie, Billy, Ba Maung and Tig Kyan joined me in studying the map. Parker wandered off to help put up a temporary hut.

Ba Maung tapped the contour lines.

66

'Here is gorge,' he said. 'Not wide – two hundred, maybe three hundred, yards – but very deep.'

'Jungle on either side,' mused Cookie.

'What's the bridge made of, Ba Maung?' asked Billy. 'Teak?'

'Teak and bamboo. Very strong.'

'But very deep,' I repeated thoughtfully. 'The right charges placed in the correct place and the whole lot will come down. It would take the Japs months to rebuild a tall structure like that.'

'Because it's so vulnerable it's bound to be well guarded,' put in Billy. 'Especially after the damage we did to the last railway line. There'll be Japs swarming all over it, just waiting for us to show up.'

I studied the map again and then pointed at another section of the railway line, about two miles away from the gorge. The line ran through jungle across the top of a plateau.

'This part won't be so heavily guarded.'

'So?' said Cookie, slightly puzzled. 'If we blow that stretch the Japs will be able to repair it in a few days. What's the point?'

'The point is it's a diversion,' I said. 'We

get Peter Simpson and his unit to set charges here while we make our way to the gorge. With a bit of luck the sound of the explosion when his charges go off will bring all the Japanese in the area rushing to the plateau, freeing the gorge for us to get at the bridge's structure.'

'And what if the Japs decide to stay and guard the bridge?' asked Billy.

I shrugged. There was no need to answer: we all knew the consequences.

Chapter 8

Into the Gorge

Three days later we arrived at the railway line. Three days of hard travelling through treacherous jungle, battling with swamps, insects and illness. By now most of us were suffering from various jungle diseases and we were all feeling weak. With our diminishing rations we also had to conserve as much as possible because we didn't know when we'd be able to arrange another supply drop. We could have tried going into a local village and bartering for food, but Captain Hayes was against it for two reasons: the first was that it would put the villagers at risk; but the second and most tactical reason was that there might be someone in the village who'd report us to the Japanese for a reward.

Captain Hayes had accepted my recommendations for blowing the bridge at the gorge, with a diversionany explosion on the nearby plateau. Peter Simpson was only too happy to take his unit and lay the explosion on the plateau. We agreed a time-frame for the operation which would give him the opportunity to get clear, and my unit to get to the bridge. Our plan was for my unit to get to the top of the ridge overlooking the gorge. When we were ready to descend it, we would signal to Peter by using mirrors. Peter would set his explosion to go off one hour after we'd signalled. By then, if we were lucky, we would be part way down the gorge. Providing the Japanese sent all their forces to investigate the explosion on the plateau, we would have approximately an hour to get to the bridge supports and set our charges.

So at dawn on the morning of the third day, Cookie, Billy, Ba Maung, Tig Kyan and Private Parker and myself lay hidden in thick bushes at the ridge that looked down on to the gorge. We were about four miles from the bridge. I studied it through my binoculars.

As we'd expected, the bridge was swarming with Japanese. Its supports were guarded by about twenty soldiers. The Japs had obviously reached the same conclusion as we had: the gorge was the most vulnerable place for the railway line to be attacked.

Cookie had also been using his binoculars.

'I've counted twenty-three soldiers down on the bed of the gorge,' he said.

'I made it twenty,' I said.

'I spotted a few more hiding in the bushes.'

'They've also got a machine-gun post down there which we'll have to deal with.'

'Twenty-three against five,' murmured Billy. 'That's not too bad!'

'That's excluding the ones on top of the bridge,' I pointed out. 'I've counted another twenty-five up there.'

'Fifty against five,' nodded Billy. 'Ten against one. Now those are the sort of odds that make it interesting.'

I took out my mirror and flashed it into the sun twice, sending my message to Peter that we were ready. At first there was no answering flash and I wondered if Peter and his unit had made it safely to the plateau. I was just about to signal again when I saw Peter's answer. So he was all set too.

'OK,' I said, 'let's go.'

We began our descent down the side of the gorge. Luckily it was covered in thick jungle, so we were able to keep under cover the whole time. It was an arduous journey, especially hauling the explosives down, because we were weak from illness and meagre rations. I kept one eye on my watch the whole time, ticking off the minutes. We needed to get to the bottom of the gorge just as Peter's explosion went off. We had to strike while the Japanese were momentarily off guard, distracted by the incident. Any delay and we would get caught by them when they returned, after they'd discovered that Peter's explosion hadn't caused much damage. We were still about half a mile from the floor of the gorge when we heard the explosion from the plateau.

By the sound of it, Peter had done a good job: a loud explosion guaranteed to attract attention. We heard shouts and yells from the soldiers on the bridge and down in the gorge. We also heard some firing coming from the soldiers guarding the approaches to the bridge.

Billy scanned the bridge through his binoculars and whispered, 'It's worked! They're all heading for the plateau!'

'All of them?' I asked.

Billy looked again.

'They've left the machine-gun crew,' he reported. 'Two men, plus I think I can see another one walking around down there.' He looked through his binoculars again and nodded. 'Yes, definitely three of them in all.'

'Me, Ba Maung and Tig Kyan will take care of them,' said Cookie.

I nodded. 'No shooting, though,' I said. 'Silently. We can't risk anything that will attract attention and bring the other guards back too soon.'

'No worries,' said Cookie grimly.

'Right. In that case, Billy, Parker, you two carry the explosives and stay with me,' I said. 'We'll let Cookie, Ba Maung and Tig Kyan take out the guards first. Then we'll

73

go to work. Cookie, Ba Maung and Tig Kyan, you keep watch while we're busy.'

They all nodded. I took a deep breath. What was it Cookie had said: that this was death or glory? Well, our moment of death or glory was upon us now.

Chapter 9

Ready to Blow

We crept through the jungle floor of the gorge. Even down there we could hear the sounds of shouting and occasionally shots on the plateau. Peter's blowing of the railway line had certainly caused the diversion we needed.

When we were within fifty yards of the bridge's base, I gestured for Billy and Parker to stay with me while Cookie, Ba Maung and Tig Kyan went ahead to deal with the guards.

Cookie and the two Burmese slipped into the bushes and disappeared. Billy, Parker and I crouched, straining our ears. We could hear the Japanese chatting. They obviously thought all the danger was up on the plateau. The talking stopped abruptly. We heard grunts, choking sounds and then silence. A quiet low whistle, like a bird. Cookie was telling us everything was clear.

Billy, Parker and I moved forward and reached the base of the bridge where the tangle of support beams was sunk into the ground. Cookie, Ba Maung and Tig Kyan were already stripping the jackets and caps from the dead soldiers and putting them on. That done, they dragged the dead bodies into the undergrowth. Now they took their positions at the machine-gun. Anyone glancing down into the gorge would see the gun manned.

I stationed Parker in the undergrowth to keep watch. Also, I didn't want him working with me while I laid the charges. Parker was very nervous and letting a jittery man handle explosives could have been fatal for all of us. Billy and I set to work, climbing up the middle support to the crucial joining section.

I set a primary charge which could be activated instantly if we were interrupted. The problem was, it would also blow us up with it. When that was set, Billy and I stuck the plastic explosive at weight-bearing points along the middle section. We ran the wires into them. Next, we set the timer pencils: three lots set to go off at five-minute intervals. This was a precaution in case one should fail. It also added to the overall damage when there was one explosion on top of another. I set the first charge to go off in forty-five minutes.

As soon as the charges were set, Billy and I clambered back down the supports as fast as we could.

'Let's go!' I whispered to Cookie, Ba Maung and Tig Kyan. They grabbed their own clothes and followed us into the jungle. As we moved they tore off their Japanese uniforms and put their own back on. It was a wise move: they didn't fancy being shot accidentally by our own boys.

We found Private Parker where we'd left him.

'I think the Japs are coming back down,' he whispered, fear in his eyes.

I looked up at the plateau through my binoculars. Parker was right. A detachment of Japanese soldiers was already heading back down into the gorge. I wondered whether we'd been spotted or if someone had just noticed that the machine-gun crew had suddenly vanished. Whatever the reason, I calculated that it would take them just over half an hour to get back. That would give them time to spot the explosives' charges and dismantle them.

'I'm going back to reset the timers,' I said.

Cookie stopped me.

'You'll never make it,' he said. 'By the time you get there the Japs will be on the bridge. They'll get you easily before you have a chance to get away.'

'I'm not going to get away,' I said grimly. 'I'll set the charges to go up instantly.'

'That's madness.' said Billy. 'You'll be blown up.'

'At least the bridge will be gone,' I said.

'I'm not going to let you do it,' said Cookie.

'Cookie, I'm going to pull rank on you,' I said. 'I'm in charge of this unit and those are my orders.'

'Forget it, Lieutenant,' said Cookie firmly. 'Make one move towards that bridge and I'll knock you out.'

'And you can count me in on that,' added Billy. 'Anyway, there's a way we can still blow the bridge without you killing yourself.'

'How?' I asked.

'We hold them down in the gorge,' answered Billy. 'Stop them getting up the supports to the detonators.'

'But we'll be killed!' protested Parker. 'Look how many of them there are! We're far outnumbered!'

I looked at the bridge and weighed up what Billy had suggested. It was possible. If we could keep them pinned down long enough, it might just work. Our only hope was that they would think we were a bigger unit than we were. If they realized there were just six of us they'd launch a full-scale attack on our position, while others disarmed the detonators. If that happened, Parker would be right. We'd be overwhelmed. However, it was the only hope we had of blowing up the bridge.

'OK,' I nodded. 'That's what we'll do.

Spread out so that once we start firing they'll think they're surrounded by a big unit.'

'This is madness!' protested Parker.

'Maybe, but it's our only option,' I said. 'Get to your positions. Hold your fire until I open up. The longer we can leave it until we let them know we're here, the better it'll be for us.'

We spread out across the floor of the gorge, each of us finding a hiding-place in the thick undergrowth. I focused my binoculars on the Japanese soldiers working their way down the side of the gorge. There were seventeen of them. The others had obviously stayed to guard the damaged railway line. I looked at my watch. Just fifteen minutes to go before the first charge went off. It would only be a matter of seconds before one of the enemy spotted that the machine-gun crew were missing, and all hell would then be let loose.

Chapter 10
Splitting Up

There was a cry of alarm from one of the Japanese soldiers. He'd spotted the empty machine-gun post. His yell brought the others running, guns levelled and ready. Soon they had uncovered the bodies of their three dead comrades. In my hiding-place I checked my watch again. The first charge was due to go off in twelve minutes. Twelve long, agonizing minutes to wait.

The Japanese spent another two minutes examining the bodies and talking excitedly, figuring out what had happened, before their officer snapped out a command to silence them. He began pacing around the machine-gun, checking for tracks. All this took another two minutes. Eight minutes before blast-off.

Suddenly one of the Japanese soldiers glanced up at the bridge supports and yelled out. Everyone looked up to where he was pointing and spotted the plastic explosive and the charges.

Immediately there was a state of panic, which was quickly brought under control by the officer. He pointed at the explosives and ordered one of his men to climb up and disarm them. I checked my watch. Six minutes to go.

The soldier looked unwilling to carry out this task, but he obeyed orders and began to climb. I let him get six feet off the ground and then I opened fire with my Thompson, as did the others. He was hit on the leg, lost his balance and fell to the ground.

The rest of his unit took cover in the bushes before they opened up with returning fire.

I looked up to the plateau. The shooting down in the gorge had attracted the attention of the other Japanese and, even as I watched, I could see them starting to return.

Four minutes to go. That was provided the timer pencils worked.

The Japanese officer shouted an order, and some of his men began to work their way towards us. A hail of bullets from our positions sent them scurrying back, although two of them fell to the ground where they stood.

The soldiers descending the side of the gorge increased their pace. If they reached the bottom before the charges went off we'd be overwhelmed by them.

I fired off another machine-gun burst. Two minutes to go.

Another man was climbing up the bridge's supports, followed by a second. They were making a determined effort to get up and disable the explosives. Meanwhile their comrades were keeping up rapid fire on us, making it difficult to get a proper aim on the two climbers.

One minute to go.

One of the climbers was only about four feet away from the first charge.

Zero . . . but nothing happened! The first timer didn't go off! That meant another five minutes before the second timer pencil detonated its charge. Five precious minutes!

The climbing soldier inched towards the explosive, his hand clawing up towards the detonator wire. In a few seconds he would be there.

Suddenly the delayed first charge went off. The soldier and the support strut he was on disappeared in a burst of flame and smoke.

'That's it!' I yelled. 'Out!'

While the Japanese soldiers looked up in horror at the bridge above them as it creaked and swayed, we began to retreat.

We headed along the gorge, away from the now tottering bridge. As we ran I heard another explosion behind us as the second timer went off. I turned. The wooden supports had broken and were falling down into the gorge like so much firewood, some of them in flames. The railway bridge, its supports weakened, was swaying like a length of twisted ribbon in the wind. And then the whole thing collapsed, tumbling down into the gorge and sending dust and smoke rising high into the air.

I rushed to join Cookie and the others heading up the steep side of the gorge. With a bit of luck the Japanese would be too occupied with the collapsing bridge to worry about giving chase to us immediately. Our mission was accomplished.

We made it back to where Captain Hayes and the rest of our column were waiting for us. Reports of our success in blowing up the bridge had already got back, and they greeted us with handshakes and hearty slaps on the back. I sought out Peter Simpson and congratulated him and his crew on their work in creating the diversionary explosion on the plateau.

'Yes, but you got the big one,' grinned Peter. 'I watched it from cover. A beautiful piece of work!'

Captain Hayes joined us.

'We've got new orders from Brigade HQ,' he said. 'Now the bridge is blown, our mission's over. Brigade HQ have ordered us back to our own lines. We are to split the column up into small units to avoid detection. The Japs will be combing every single yard of the jungle and a whole column would soon be spotted.' Hayes turned and looked at us. 'That's it, chaps. Small units, and I'm afraid the only supplies are those you have with you right now. Brigade HQ can't chance another drop. So, do your best not to get caught. And with a bit of luck, we'll see each other in India.'

I turned to look at Billy. The excitement from having completed our mission successfully had left him. His face reflected the reality of our present predicament. Here we were, hundreds of miles from our own lines, with thick jungle in between. Our rations were low, so was our ammo. We were tired and weak. And on top of all this, 80,000 Japanese soldiers were looking for us, with express orders not to take prisoners but to kill on sight.

Chapter 11
Homeward Bound

For the first time on this campaign I was completely responsible for the men of my unit. I decided on a democratic approach to our withdrawal. I may have been the expert when it came to blowing things up, but Cookie and Billy were more experienced jungle hands than me, and Ba Maung and Tig Kyan even more so in this particular area. As the rest of our column dispersed, I sat down, unfolded my map and held a council of war with my men.

'Right,' I said. 'As officer in charge I'll take any final decisions, but as all our lives are at risk, and you chaps are better in the jungle than me, I want your suggestions about how we can get out of here quickly and safely.'

Cookie, Billy, Ba Maung and Tig Kyan studied the map. Private Parker hung about on the edge of the clearing, nervous, his Lee-Enfield rifle held ready, expecting the Japanese to attack us at any moment.

I traced two routes on the map.

'The shortest route is due west, back across the Irrawaddy where it's widest and then up to the Indian border. The longer route is due north up into China, crossing the Irrawaddy where it's narrow. Whichever one we take we also have to cross the Chindwin.'

'The Japs are bound to be watching the Irrawaddy,' said Cookie. 'So crossing it where it's wide is going to be difficult: we'll be an easy target. That's assuming we can borrow a boat, which will put its owners at risk. Word will also get back to the Japanese, letting them know our position.'

'On the other hand, if we head north it will add days to our journey,' Billy pointed out. 'And we don't have the rations.'

'What about living off the jungle?' I asked, looking at Cookie.

Cookie laughed.

'Yes and no,' he said. 'We can get some

food from it, but not in bulk. Not for six of us.'

'So long as we can find enough to give us the strength to keep moving,' I said.

We pored over the map for another ten minutes, with suggestions being made by Ba Maung and Tig Kyan about the different kinds of jungle we would be passing through on either route. Finally, after weighing up all the pros and cons, I made a decision.

'The logical choice, if we had sufficient rations, would be to strike north for China. The Japs don't know we're short of food, so my guess is that's the way they think we'll be heading. So, we'll go west. The enemy are watching for us everywhere. I'm hoping that we can catch them by surprise. They won't think anyone would be so foolish as to try and cross the Irrawaddy a second time. Once we're across –'

'If we get across,' grumbled Parker.

'Once we're across,' I repeated firmly, 'we take the shortest route to the Chindwin. Split up as we are, we've got a very good chance of making it, because with a bit of luck the Japanese won't be able to cope with chasing all the separate units.'

Cookie gave another grin.

'Always the optimist,' he laughed. 'What happens if we get the bad luck and all the Japs suddenly come after *us*?'

'In that case we'll be outnumbered about eighty thousand to six,' I grinned back. 'And we'll be running so fast we won't have time to worry about it.' I folded the map up and put it in my pack. 'Right,' I said, 'let's get going. We've got three hundred miles of hard travelling.'

And so we began our journey back. I decided to try another bold tactic, one which had worked successfully after we'd ambushed the train, and which I hoped the Japanese would think as too lunatic and dangerous for us to try: we used the road. However, to cut down our chances of being caught, we marched at night. My thinking on this was that we would see the headlights of any approaching vehicles and so could take cover.

Travelling by night also gave us further protection. It would be difficult for a patrol to identify our uniforms. I hoped the

Japanese would assume that any body of men marching boldly along a road couldn't possibly be British.

In this way, travelling along the road by night and hiding under cover in the jungle during the day, we made good time. Three days later we were within twenty miles of the Irrawaddy without once having come face to face with any Japanese.

We'd been aware of them, though. A couple of times while hiding in the jungle we'd smelt the smoke from fires, which could have meant a Japanese camp not far away. With our declining rations the temptation to attack the camp and take some food had been hard to resist, but we tightened our belts and stayed put.

We'd also heard some shooting and guessed that the Japanese had stumbled on one of the other units returning home. I only hoped that they had made it.

The last stretch to the Irrawaddy was through thick jungle. We stumbled and squelched through swamp much of the time, our guns held above our heads to keep them dry. The trees seemed to close in on us and we had to hack our way through them for many miles, the muscles of our arms sore and aching from swinging our machetes.

With darkness starting to fall, we came to the edge of the jungle where the mud bank ran down to the Irrawaddy. The river was too wide and the current too strong for us to swim across.

We worked our way along the bank, keeping to the cover of the jungle, looking for a place where the river might be narrower, a boat might have been left, or where a stretch of sand bank might lessen the gap. We trekked cautiously for two miles, our eyes on the river but our ears alert for any sounds of enemy troops, and taking turns on point.

I was taking my turn at second point, just behind Cookie, when he stopped and raised a hand. I crept forward to join him. We peered through the trees. There, at the river's edge, were two bamboo huts in front of a landing stage. Flying above them was a Japanese flag. From inside, we could hear voices.

Chapter 12
The River

Billy, Ba Maung, Tig Kyan and Parker caught us up. We crouched in the jungle and surveyed the huts. I could see four armed Japanese soldiers on guard duty. I guessed there would be at least another four inside the huts, maybe more. I looked through my binoculars at the opposite bank and motioned Billy and Cookie to do the same.

'Well?' I whispered.

'There's another small encampment over there, hidden just inside the trees,' said Billy, keeping his voice low.

'That's what I thought,' I nodded in agreement. 'From the number of huts I can make out, I doubt if there are more than eight Japanese over there.'

'Ten,' said Cookie. 'I can see them.'

'OK, ten on that bank, about the same here.'

'And a boat,' said Billy, pointing.

We all looked harder. We could just see the end of a boat hidden behind the huts.

'It doesn't look much,' commented Parker.

'Right at this moment, anything bigger than a rubber duck is better than nothing,' Billy told him.

I eased further back in the trees and then moved along the bank so I could get a better view of the boat.

'It's large enough to take us,' I said.

'Where, straight into the Japs on the other side?' asked Parker acidly.

'No, downriver,' I said.

'Down?' queried Cookie. 'I thought we were trying to head north.'

'Do you fancy trying to paddle against the current while those Japs on the other bank are shooting at us?' I asked him.

Cookie saw what I was getting at and grinned.

'Point taken, boss,' he said.

My plan was to snatch the boat and use

the current to take us downriver at speed, letting the river carry us while we kept our hands free to fire at the Japs on the other bank. Once we were a safe distance downstream, we'd head over to the opposite bank. But first we had to get hold of the boat. And to do that we had to get past the Japanese.

I gave my orders in a whisper, and then we set off towards the bamboo huts. Fortunately for us, the guards on duty had got complacent. I suppose they didn't think that anyone would try anything so foolish as to attempt to cross a river where there was a fortified Japanese post.

Cookie and Ba Maung crept through the trees right up to where the mud began. Billy and I kept our tommy-guns trained on the two guards, just in case anything should go wrong.

Cookie and Ba Maung disappeared from our sight, taking cover behind thick bushes near the huts.

The guards made their patrol, their route taking them right by the bushes.

Cookie and Ba Maung struck in a flash, leaping up and pulling the two guards down behind the bushes. There was hardly a sound. Then Cookie appeared and gave me a thumbs-up sign.

I motioned Billy, Tig Kyan and Parker to follow me, and we crept over to join Cookie and Ba Maung. The two guards on the landing stage hadn't heard a thing. They stood, looking up and down the river.

I whispered my orders.

'Billy and Parker, you take the first hut. Cookie and Tig Kyan, you take the other. Ba Maung and I will take out the guards on the river.'

I did a countdown on my upheld fingers to give them their cue: three – two – one . . .

We sprang up and moved. Billy kicked in the door of the first hut and leapt in, his gun blazing. Cookie did the same to the second hut, the sound of their guns tearing into the jungle stillness.

Ba Maung and I were already running past the huts, our guns firing as the two Japanese soldiers on the landing stage turned in surprise.

The noise of our attack had already roused the soldiers on the far bank and I could see them pouring out of the jungle towards the river, guns at the ready.

Cookie, Billy, Parker and Tig Kyan joined us on the landing stage.

'Into the boat!' I ordered.

I hardly needed to say it. Billy was already untying the mooring rope. A few seconds later we were on our way, the boat rocking and turning, caught in the fast current of the river, while we kept firing at the Japanese on the opposite bank.

The soldiers on the far side were running along the mud flats, trying to keep up with us. A hail of bullets ripped into the boat, tearing off splinters of wood and metal.

Suddenly the craft lurched violently. It had clipped a rock. I heard a yell behind me and I turned, just in time to see Parker topple into the water with an expression of horror on his face. He clutched desperately for help as the current swept him away.

Chapter 13
Casualties of War

'Cover me!' I shouted to the others.

I grabbed the mooring rope and jumped into the river.

I swam towards Parker as fast as I could and just managed to catch up with him as he went down. He bobbed back to the surface, gasping for air.

'Here!' I yelled, and thrust the rope towards him.

Parker grabbed it with one hand and then disappeared under the surface of the water again.

'Haul him in!' I shouted at the boat.

Ba Maung was already pulling on the rope while Cookie, Billy and Tig Kyan kept up covering fire.

I dived under the surface and felt the

fast-moving current whirl me around. Reaching out, I felt my hands touch Parker's clothes. I gripped them and kicked back to the surface again. With one hand under Parker's chin, I held his head above the water as Ba Maung pulled him in to the boat.

By now Tig Kyan was using a paddle he'd found to take us towards the far bank.

Ba Maung reached down and grabbed Parker by the collar and held him half out of the water as the boat headed into the shallows. I hauled myself up on to the edge of the boat and let myself be dragged along with it. The current had carried us quite a distance. The Japanese soldiers were still coming after us. We could hear them crashing through the jungle towards our position.

The boat slid aground on the muddy riverbank.

'Out!' I yelled.

Cookie, Billy and Tig Kyan leapt on to the bank and ran into the jungle to defend our position, while Ba Maung and I dragged the half-conscious Parker across the mud.

'Here they come!' yelled Billy.

The Japanese soldiers came into view through the trees, their guns blazing bullets at us. Cookie, Billy and Tig Kyan were already firing back. Ba Maung and I dropped Parker facedown on to the ground. While Ba Maung snatched his gun and joined the fight, I worked on Parker, pressing on his back and pushing the water out of his lungs until he began to cough and splutter.

Reassured that Parker was alive and would recover, I turned and ran back towards the boat, squelching through the mud. Having retrieved my tommy-gun, I returned to the battle. The fire from the Japanese hidden in the trees was dying down. We were winning.

And then I saw Billy fall, his gun dropped to the ground.

I let fly with a long burst, as did the others, and the shooting from the Japs stopped.

While Ba Maung, Tig Kyan and I moved forward, guns at the ready, into the trees, Cookie went to check on Billy.

Six Japanese soldiers lay dead in the

jungle. That meant the others had stayed back at their camp and were probably radioing our position to their HQ.

I hurried back to see how Billy was.

Cookie was kneeling over him. Billy didn't move; he just lay there, a pool of blood staining the grass beneath him. Cookie stood up and shook his head, a look of deep pain on his young face.

'Billy took a hit in the neck.' He paused, then added: 'He's dead.'

Chapter 14
Trapped

Cookie and I looked down at our comrade. This boy of nineteen had come all the way from Kenya to fight for his home country, and now he had died out here in the jungle of south-east Asia. I felt a deep sense of sadness and loss. I'd lost friends before in this war, but Cookie, Billy and I had been together since we'd first started our commando training the year before. But there was no time to dwell on the past.

'Take his rations, weapons and ammo,' I said. 'We have to move on fast. Jap reinforcements will be on their way.'

While Cookie took Billy's equipment, I went to see how Parker was doing. The private was on his feet, still coughing and soaked to the skin.

'We have to move on,' I said.

'I understand, sir,' he said.

I was a little surprised by his behaviour, expecting a complaint of some sort about nearly drowning. I was even more amazed when he held out his hand to me.

'Thank you, sir,' he said. 'You saved my life. I didn't think you would. Don't you lot just leave your blokes behind if anything happens to them?'

I took his hand and shook it.

'Not if there's a chance to save someone,' I said.

I let his hand go and gestured at Billy.

'I'm afraid not everyone can be saved,' I said sadly.

Parker looked at Billy and nodded.

'I'm sorry,' he replied. 'I know he was your pal.'

'He was,' I replied, too choked with emotion to say anything else.

Cookie had now distributed Billy's belongings between himself, Ba Maung and Tig Kyan.

'Ready,' he told me.

'OK,' I said. 'Let's get going!'

We spent the next six days on the move,

stopping only to snatch a few hours' sleep in deep cover in the jungle when we could, taking turns to keep watch.

I guessed that the Japanese would expect us to head north or due west and that they'd concentrate their search for us in those areas. Instead, after leaving the crossing point we took a diversionary route south along the river for ten miles before turning west. It added more time to our journey and made a greater demand on our precious few rations, but I hoped it would stop us running into another Japanese patrol.

By now we were all getting thinner and weaker. We were driving ourselves on with adrenalin and a fierce determination to get back to our own lines. No longer in radio contact with Brigade HQ, we had no idea how the rest of the units were doing – if any of them had made it back yet, or if they'd been caught. All we could do was hack our way through the jungle, battling with swamps and insects, and doing our best to be as quiet as possible as we made our way. By now our map was useless. We were so far off any track, my compass and the sun were our only guides to the direction in which we were heading.

After six days of taking an erratic course, doubling back on ourselves and laying false trails to throw any pursuer off our scent, we finally made it to the Chindwin. Only this time the river was heavily patrolled by Japanese.

We crouched in the jungle and I surveyed the river through binoculars. There was a large bamboo hut, presumably the command post, and several smaller ones dotted at intervals along the bank. Enemy patrols covered the area. Machine-gun posts had been set up at intervals. The river bank was now a fortified front line. After the attacks we'd made on them behind their own lines, the Japanese had thrown a net along the whole length of the Chindwin, determined to catch as many of us Chindits as they could. And right now we were caught in that net. We couldn't go forward, and we couldn't go back. It was frustrating to have come so far, to be so near to our own lines.

'Any ideas?' asked Cookie.

'Our only hope is that our own troops

are watching on the other side of the river,' I said. 'If we can get part of the way across, they might be able to give us covering fire.'

'It's a big "if",' said Cookie. 'We've been out of contact for so long we don't know what the situation is. For all we know the Japs may have taken both sides of the river.'

Reluctantly, I had to admit that Cookie could well be right.

'I'm afraid it's a chance we're going to have to take,' I said. 'We can't go back, and we're certainly not going to surrender. Remember, the Japs have orders to kill any of us they catch.'

'So we go across,' nodded Cookie. 'Where?'

'I suppose we have to look for the weak spot in the net,' I said.

We spent the rest of that day crawling through the jungle, keeping parallel to the Chindwin, looking for a gap that we could make a dash through and get to the river. We didn't find one. The Japanese had learnt from their previous river encounters with us and had a tight line of defence. Our other problem was that, even if we did make it to the river, we didn't have any way of getting across except by swimming. And swimming across the strong Chindwin would be fatal: we all risked being sucked under and drowned.

Early the next morning, as dawn broke, we were still working our way slowly through the riverside jungle, searching for an escape route. It was Tig Kyan who spotted one. A number of logs had been felled at the edge of the jungle in readiness for building more guard huts. They had fallen so that they were almost in the water.

'There,' said Tig. 'We use logs as boats.'

'We'll never get them into the water without a patrol seeing us,' said Parker doubtfully. 'Just look at the length of them. We're talking very heavy logs. It'd take all five of us just to push one.'

'The mud will help us,' I said. 'They'll slide.'

'On the other hand, they might sink into it and stick firm,' said Cookie.

'And we'll be sitting ducks,' I admitted. 'But those logs are the only chance we've got to get across that river.'

We studied the scene. A Japanese patrol

guarded the area where the fallen logs lay. Another patrol of seven soldiers was stationed a hundred yards upriver by one of the small huts, with yet another patrol the same distance downriver from the logs.

'We need a diversion,' Cookie said. 'Something to attract their attention while we get to the logs.'

I thought it over, then I announced:

'I'll blow up the main hut.'

'You'll never get near enough to plant your charges,' Cookie pointed out. 'Anyway, we've got no plastic explosive left.'

'I'll do it the old-fashioned way,' I said, and produced a hand-grenade from my pack. 'We've got four of these left. I'll throw three of them at one-minute intervals at the hut. The first should bring the Japs by the logs running. The second should keep them down, wondering where the next attack is coming from. I'll let drop my third one into the hut while you, Cookie, chuck our last grenade at the Jap patrol downriver. Once the grenades have gone off, Cookie and I will just keep firing at the Japs to keep them down.

'While all this is going on, Parker, Ba

Maung and Tig Kyan, you get yourselves ready near the bank. As the last grenade goes off, push one of the logs into the river. Cookie and I will join you, so you'd better choose one big enough to take the weight of all five of us.'

'Not that any of us weigh that much any more!' laughed Cookie.

'When do we move?' asked Tig.

'We wait until dark,' I said. 'No sense in letting the Japs have clear aim at us in daylight.'

'If one of us loses his grip on the log in the river in the dark, we won't be able to see him to save him,' Cookie pointed out.

I shrugged.

'True,' I said, 'but this is our only option. So we'll just have to hang on as tightly as we can, and kick hard towards the opposite bank.'

'And hope we're not swimming right into Japanese hands,' said Parker gloomily.

Chapter 15

Back Across the Chindwin

We stayed hidden in the jungle until darkness fell. I spent the time planning my path through the trees to the target hut. Once I'd lobbed the grenades, I knew I had the difficult task of getting out of the jungle and along the top of the mud bank to join up with Parker, Ba Maung and Tig Kyan. There were so many things that could go wrong. The log could stick and sink in the mud. The grenades might have got damaged on our trip. The moon might suddenly come out from behind cloud and light us up as if it was broad daylight. Or it might be so dark that we missed each other. My only hope was that Cookie and I would cause so much confusion with our grenades and gunfire that the Japs would be running around in panic, thinking they were under attack from the jungle, and not realize what we were doing.

Two hours later, darkness fell. We could just see one or two of the soldiers still standing at the river's edge. Most of the other guards upriver had returned to the main hut, and those downriver had gathered round a small fire. It sent out a glow which would help them to spot us. On the other hand, if Cookie was able to place his grenade close to the fire to blow the burning embers over the soldiers, it would cause even more panic and confusion. I suggested this to him, and he nodded.

'It's going to be difficult, though,' I said. 'You'll have to get pretty close to be accurate.'

'No worries,' he said. 'You should have seen me playing cricket back in Oz. I was a devil in the outfield. I could hit the stumps from a hundred yards.'

'Let's hope your aim's still as good,' I grinned. 'OK, Parker, Ba Maung and Tig Kyan, work your way down towards the river. As soon as the action goes off, run

111

for the river. And once you get that log afloat, start kicking water. Don't wait for us.' I grimaced ruefully. 'And just in case we don't make it, good luck. You've been a great bunch of blokes to work with. The best.'

With that, Cookie and I headed off to our own targets, while the rest made their way to the water's edge.

As I crept through the trees my mind went back to my first jungle-training exercise, when Sergeant Ross had caught me. I remembered what I had learnt that night from him, and from many other nights afterwards. Merge with the jungle. Be part of it. Be an extension of the trees, the bushes, the mud, the air. Move like an animal does when it's stalking its prey, slowly, all senses alert, but silent, invisible.

I crept nearer and nearer to the hut. The clouds broke enough for moonlight to shine through. Then they covered the moon and it was dark again.

I was within throwing distance now. My first throw had to be accurate. I had to make sure it went between the trees and into the hut. The last thing I wanted was for the grenade to hit a branch and bounce back at me.

Through the gloom I could make out the shape of one of the guards, strolling away from the hut, continuing his patrol. I took my first grenade, pulled out the pin, counted down . . . and then threw it. It soared through the trees and landed just beside the hut with a soft thud. The sentry turned. As he headed back towards the hut, the grenade went off.

Immediately there was panic and confusion. There were yells and shouts from inside the hut as the bamboo caught fire. Soldiers stumbled out on to the mud bank, grabbing their weapons. I counted down the seconds . . . 20 . . . 15 . . . 10 . . . before I lobbed my second grenade. Its blast hurled some of the soldiers back into the jungle.

Already the Japanese from downriver were running towards the spot, yelling and shouting, guns all over the place as they looked for any sign of the attackers.

I lobbed my third grenade right into the crowd of soldiers now gathered around the burning hut. It went off with devastating effect. At the same time I heard the explosion further downriver from Cookie's grenade. Then I began my run towards where I hoped that Parker, Ba Maung and Tig Kyan had managed to get the log into the water.

I squelched through the mud, sinking as I ran. I could barely make out the figures of Parker, Ba Maung and Tig Kyan up to their waists in water, pushing the log away from the bank. Cookie was with them too. I was about to make it into the water when a sudden pain tore through my right leg and I went down. Bullets tore into the mud around me.

I tried to get to my feet, but my right leg gave way and I just sank back down again, an incredible pain shooting right up through my body. Then another bullet thudded into my shoulder, knocking me flat into the mud. My tommy-gun fell out of my hands. Frantically I reached for it, but it was too far away. Footsteps were approaching me now. All I could do was wait to be killed. Then a figure loomed over me.

'Come on, Lieutenant,' said Parker, 'the last boat is waiting.'

'Go on without me!' I shouted. 'That's an order!'

'You can court-martial me when we get home,' answered Parker.

He dragged me along the mud towards the river. The pain in my leg and shoulder was incredible. Then I felt the water lapping around me as we waded into the Chindwin.

As we arrived at the log, I saw the figure of Cookie standing waist deep in the river, tommy-gun levelled, and he let off a long burst of fire.

'That should keep them busy!' he snapped.

I bumped against the floating log and reached with my good arm to grab on to a cut-off branch protruding from it.

Cookie and Parker hauled themselves half out of the water on to the log, lying flat across it, while keeping a grip on my uniform, helping to hold me steady.

'Kick!' yelled Cookie.

Behind us the firing continued. Bullets fizzed into the water around us, now and then one thudding into the log. But it was too dark and we were moving too fast with the current for them to get a clear shot.

When we were over halfway across I wondered if more Japanese were waiting for us on the other side. Suddenly our worst fears were realized, because gunfire opened up from the trees opposite.

'We're finished!' yelled Parker.

'No!' shouted Cookie. 'They're not shooting at us! They're our blokes giving us covering fire!'

The pain in my shoulder and leg had gone, and had been replaced by a deep numbness. I could sense I was about to lose consciousness and began to slip off the log. But the grip on my clothes tightened.

'Hang on, John!' came Cookie's voice. 'We're nearly there!'

Then the log lurched as the end ran aground on the mud. I found myself momentarily floating free, before being dragged up the bank.

'Well, well,' murmured a Scottish voice that I recognized. 'So you survived after all, Lieutenant!'

'Thanks to Private Parker,' I said.

With that, I was lifted on to a stretcher. As I was taken away I managed to lift my right hand in a thumbs-up to Cookie, Ba Maung, Tig Kyan and Private Parker. In the faint moonlight I saw them all smile back at me.

We had done it. We'd completed our mission. And we'd made it back home.

The 1943 Chindit Campaign

Of the 3,000 Chindits who went into Burma in February 1943, about 2,000 made it back to India. During the campaign they had travelled over 1,000 miles through treacherous jungle. In reality they were ordered to disperse and withdraw before they could carry out some of their objectives. However, the Chindits caused major disruptions in Burma, including cutting other supply lines to the Japanese front-line forces.

Early in 1944 the second Chindit campaign was launched, from the west, into Burma with a much larger force of 23,000 men in six brigades. At the same time, another Chindit-style guerrilla attack behind Japanese lines was launched by the Americans in the north of Burma. These American guerrillas were known as Merrill's Marauders after their commander, Brigadier-General Frank Merrill. They initially attacked both by air and by jungle penetration. They were part of an overall campaign to recapture Burma, combined with traditional frontal assaults by British, American and Chinese troops.

Caught on all sides, the Japanese forces, under General Mutaguchi, fought hard to defend their positions. But on 8 July 1944 General Mutaguchi ordered their retreat. Additional British, American and Chinese forces were poured in as the Allied offensive increased. By February 1945 Allied forces had taken most of Burma. The capital, Rangoon, was finally taken by units of General Messervy's British IV Corps on 6 May 1945. This signalled the end of the war in Burma.

Orde Wingate himself was killed at the start of the second Chindit campaign, when his B-25 bomber crashed into the Burmese jungle on 24 March 1944.

What Happened Next . . .

The Long Range Penetration offensive into Burma by Wingate's Chindits had a three-fold effect:

• It showed that British troops could defeat the Japanese in jungle fighting, something that had been considered impossible. The military establishment had previously seen the Japanese as invincible in this area of combat.

• It persuaded the reluctant Americans to put more military resources into a future guerrilla campaign in Burma, which, in fact, took place in 1944.

• It led to the Japanese bringing more of their forces into Burma to oppose similar attacks, so weakening their defences else-where on the Pacific front. Japanese leaders later admitted that this factor con-tributed to their eventual defeat.

'The Commando Catechism'

(written by Lieutenant-Colonel Newman, Commanding Officer of 2 Commando, in 1941)

1 The object of Special Service is to have available a fully trained body of first-class soldiers, ready for active offensive operations against an enemy in any part of the world.

2 Irregular warfare demands the highest standards of initiative, mental alertness and physical fitness, together with the maximum skill at arms. No Commando can feel confident of success unless all ranks are capable of thinking for themselves; of thinking quickly and of acting independently, and with sound tactical sense, when faced by circumstances which may be entirely different to those which were anticipated.

3 *Mentally.* The offensive spirit must be the outlook of all ranks of a Commando at all times.

4 *Physically.* The highest state of physical fitness must at all times be maintained. All ranks are trained to cover at great speed any type of ground for distances of five to seven miles in fighting order.

5 Cliff and mountain climbing and really difficult slopes climbed quickly form a part of Commando training.

6 A high degree of skill in all branches of unarmed combat will be attained.

7 *Seamanship and Boatwork.* All ranks must be skilled in all forms of boatwork and landing-craft, whether by day or by night, as a result of which training the sea comes to be regarded as a natural working ground for a Commando.

8 Night sense and night confidence are essential. All ranks will be highly trained in the use of the compass.

9 Map reading and route memorizing form an important part of Commando training.

10 All ranks of a Commando will be trained in semaphore, Morse and the use of W/T (radio).

11 All ranks will have elementary knowledge of demolition and sabotage. All ranks will be confident in the handling of all types of high explosives, Bangalore torpedoes, and be able to set up all types of booby traps.

12 A high standard of training will be maintained in all forms of street fighting, occupation of towns, putting towns into a state of defence and the overcoming of all types of obstacles – wire, rivers, high walls, etc.

13 All ranks in a Commando should be able to drive motorcycles, cars, lorries, tracked vehicles, trains and motorboats.

14 A degree of efficiency in all forms of field-craft will be attained. Any man in a Commando must be able to forage for himself, cook and live under a bivouac for a considerable period.

15 All ranks are trained in first aid and will be capable of dealing with the dressing of gunshot wounds and the carrying of the wounded.

16 These are few among the many standards of training that must be attained during service in a Commando. At all times a high standard of discipline is essential, and the constant desire by all ranks to be fitter and better trained than anyone else.

17 The normal mode of living is that the Special Service soldier will live in a billet found by himself and fed by the billet for which he will receive 6s. 8d. (about 33p) per day to pay all his expenses.

18 Any falling short of the standards of training and behaviour on the part of a Special Service soldier will render him liable to be returned to his unit.

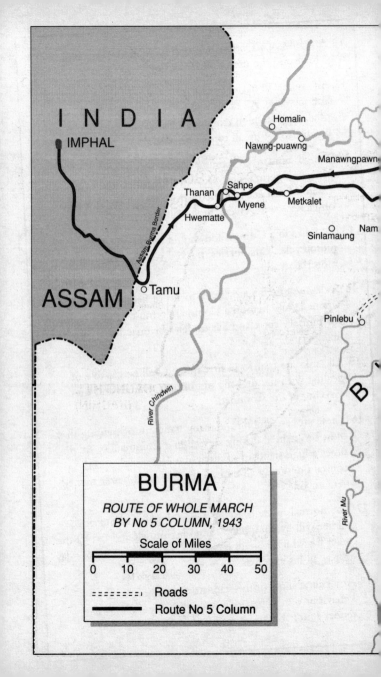

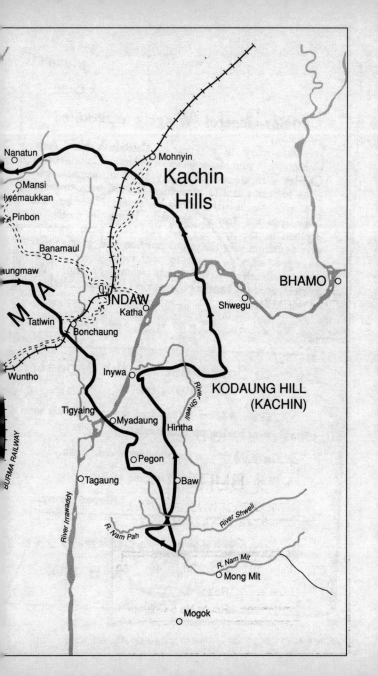

K.H4185-5

C. 221.

Major-General Wingate was killed

According to a report of the South East Asia Command, your Commander-in-chief, Major-general Charles Wingate was miserably killed in action. He came to Burma as if to be killed. Here we warn you that you will be killed like this desperate Major-general. Now you are like an aeroplane losing its motor or orphans in the jungle. The Japanese Forces want to save you from your dangerous position and to give you an opportunity to return to your sweet home. Your counter-offensives have already come to end. We advice you, in the name of Bushido (Japanese chivalry,) to surrender to the Japanese Forces.

The Japanese Forces.

How to Surrender to the Japanese Forces

1. The surrenderers are required to come hoisting some white cloth or holding up both hands.

2. Carry the rifle on the shoulder upside down.

3. Show this bill to the Japanese soldier.

Nippon Army.

此ノ證携行者ハ投降者ニツキ保護ヲ加ヘラレタシ

大 日 本 軍

Japanese propaganda leaflet dropped on Allied troops

Jungle Lore

- Whenever possible, sleep off the ground. Brushwood makes an excellent couch. Sleep under a mosquito net whenever possible. If not, use repellents.

- The cries of birds, monkeys and squirrels give warning of human movement. Use them to detect enemy movement. When YOU move, be silent.

- Never blunder through jungle; part your way. In primary jungle the ground is reasonably clear. If you stoop, you can move fast.

- For a distant view in primary jungle, bend down and look along the floor.

- If lost, keep your head. If you go downhill you will come to a stream. Follow a stream and you will reach native habitation. If lost at night choose suitable cover, away from the trail, and lie up until daylight.

- If held up by a swamp, make swamp-shoes, similar to snow-shoes, out of branches, reeds, or saplings. These will distribute weight over a greater area and permit a crossing of soft ground.

Excerpts from Practical Hints for Jungle Soldiers

What was it actually like to be in a submarine during the Second World War? Watch out for the next *Warpath* book, *Depth-charge Danger*.

KERBOOOOOSHHHHH!

The force of the exploding depth charge violently hurled our submarine sideways. I grabbed frantically on to the periscope housing, to stop myself being thrown against the metal walls.

Commander Walters gestured for everyone to stay silent. We knew that, above us, the two German ships would be listening in with their hydrophones.

No one dared move in case we made a noise.

Kerbooooshhhhh!

Another explosion, but further away this time. The submarine rocked as the force of the blast pushed us backwards through the water.

Chief Stannard, our Petty Officer, winked at me confidently. I didn't feel so optimistic. Here I was, Lieutenant John Smith, twenty years old, on my third voyage in the submarine *Sandtail*, trapped between the Germans sixty feet above and the icy depths below. My first two voyages had been without major incident. We'd gone home empty-handed after the first, and had sunk two tankers on the second. This third trip we had ventured even further, almost up to the Norwegian coast, where we'd had major successes, sinking four supply ships.

In retaliation, the Germans had sent out spotter planes and anti-submarine craft to look for us. Two hours earlier a Dornier bomber had spotted us cruising just below the surface of the water and had dropped depth charges on us. The charges had been set too deep. In one way this was fortunate, because they exploded far beneath us. However, the explosions were strong enough to push the sub sharply to the surface. Our No. 1, Derek Anderson, flooded all our tanks with ballast as fast as he could, to keep us beneath the surface of

the water, but it was no good. We had
come up, and the Dornier returned to
finish the job.

Warpath 1: Tank Attack

by J. Eldridge

In ten minutes enemy tanks are going to outnumber you five to one. What would YOU do?

July 1942 – The Allies face defeat in North Africa. Under the command of Montgomery, they make their final stand. A young tank-driver prepares for action in what was to become known as the Battle of El Alamein.

Part war story, part fact book, *Tank Attack* reveals what it was really like to drive a tank and fight in the desert.

Warpath 2: Deadly Skies

by J. Eldridge

The cockpit quickly fills with smoke. You have thirty seconds to escape death. What would YOU do?

August 1940 – Britain stands alone against the might of the Nazi blitzkrieg. Across the English Channel, just twenty miles away, enemy forces prepare to invade. For one young pilot the Battle of Britain is about to begin.

Part war story, part fact book, *Deadly Skies* reveals what it was really like to fly a plane and fight in the Battle of Britain.

READ MORE IN PUFFIN

For children of all ages, Puffin represents quality and variety – the very best in publishing today around the world.

For complete information about books available from Puffin – and Penguin – and how to order them, contact us at the appropriate address below. Please note that for copyright reasons the selection of books varies from country to country.

On the worldwide web: www.penguin.co.uk

In the United Kingdom: Please write to *Dept. EP, Penguin Books Ltd, Bath Road, Harmondsworth, West Drayton, Middlesex UB7 0DA*

In the United States: Please write to *Penguin Putnam inc., P.O. Box 12289, Dept B, Newark, New Jersey 07101-5289* or call 1-800-788-6262

In Canada: Please write to *Penguin Books Canada Ltd, 10 Alcorn Avenue, Suite 300, Toronto, Ontario M4V 3B2*

In Australia: Please write to *Penguin Books Australia Ltd, P.O. Box 257, Ringwood, Victoria 3134*

In New Zealand: Please write to *Penguin Books (NZ) Ltd, Private Bag 102902, North Shore Mail Centre, Auckland 10*

In India: Please write to *Penguin Books India Pvt Ltd, 11 Panscheel Shopping Centre, Panscheel Park, New Delhi 110 017*

In the Netherlands: Please write to *Penguin Books Netherlands bv, Postbus 3507, NL-1001 AH Amsterdam*

In Germany: Please write to *Penguin Books Deutschland GmbH, Metzlerstrasse 26, 60594 Frankfurt am Main*

In Spain: Please write to *Penguin Books S. A., Bravo Murillo 19, 1° B, 28015 Madrid*

In Italy: Please write to *Penguin Italia s.r.l., Via Felice Casati 20, I–20124 Milano*

In France: Please write to *Penguin France S. A., 17 rue Lejeune, F–31000 Toulouse*

In Japan: Please write to *Penguin Books Japan, Ishikiribashi Building, 2–5–4, Suido, Bunkyo-ku, Tokyo 112*

In South Africa: Please write to *Longman Penguin Southern Africa (Pty) Ltd, Private Bag X08, Bertsham 2013*